COMIC COLLECTION

by Tristan Demers

Scholastic Inc.

ISBN 978-1-338-14857-2

10 9 8 7 6 5 4 3 2 1   17 18 19 20 21

Printed in the U.S.A.   40

First printing 2017

Book design by Erin McMahon and Ben Mautner

SHOPKINS are bursting with imagination and creativity. They're always ready to organize crazy contests, awesome activities, and fantastic surprise parties. Travel through the Fruit & Veg, Bakery, and Sweet Treats aisles to go behind the scenes of **SMALL MART**.

Join Apple Blossom, Strawberry Kiss, Wobbles, Sally Shakes, Kooky Cookie, and their friends in adventures big and small. There's a lot to discover at the Small Mart—**LET'S GO!**

MEET THE
Shopkins

SPILT MILK

Spilt Milk is shy and a little clumsy, but she's the best friend you could ever have! She loves to stay cool on her own shelf, but she always pays a visit to her friends in other aisles.

GRAN JAM

Gran Jam has the best advice when it comes to recipes. She knows all the shelves of the supermarket by heart and the Shopkins always go to her when they need help. Her strawberry and rhubarb jam is the best in Shopville!

PAPA TOMATO

Papa Tomato has an answer for everything, probably because he always asks the best questions! He's a real legend in the supermarket. If you believe what they say, he's been there the longest—he loves to share stories from the good old days!

APPLE BLOSSOM

Apple Blossom is full of energy, and she's always ready to share some of it with her friends! She has the best ideas, and plans the most awesome parties for all of Shopville.

LIPPY LIPS

Lippy Lips can be a little sassy, but she's happiest when she sees her friends succeed. She loves shopping and polishing her acting chops.

CHEE ZEE

Chee Zee always brings a smile to his friends' faces, even though he's a little crackers! This little cheese loves to laugh and his imagination goes into overdrive whenever someone asks him to come up with a new game.

STRAWBERRY KISS

What would the Small Mart be without the sweetest Strawberry Kiss? Gentle, kind, and generous—it's impossible to resist this adorable berry!

D'LISH DONUT

A little ray of sunshine, D'Lish Donut always brightens the day of anyone she meets. Thanks to a good sense of humor and lots of energy, she'll find a solution to any problem!

CHEEKY CHOCOLATE

Did someone pull a prank on you? Look no further: It's usually the sneaky Cheeky Chocolate, the Shopkin behind any joke! Not only is she a big prankster, she loves competition and works hard to win first place in any contest!

POSH PEAR

Ooh la la, there's no one classier than Posh Pear! This serious fashionista never misses a chance to cause a sensation at the supermarket with her one-of-a-kind style. Every detail matters!

CUPCAKE QUEEN

There's no doubt that Cupcake Queen is true royalty! Her parties are her crowning achievement. If you find yourself invited to one, you'll see there's nothing else like it!

SUGAR LUMP

How can you not smile at this adorable little baby full of sweetness? Sugar Lump is known as one of the cutest Shopkins around.

9

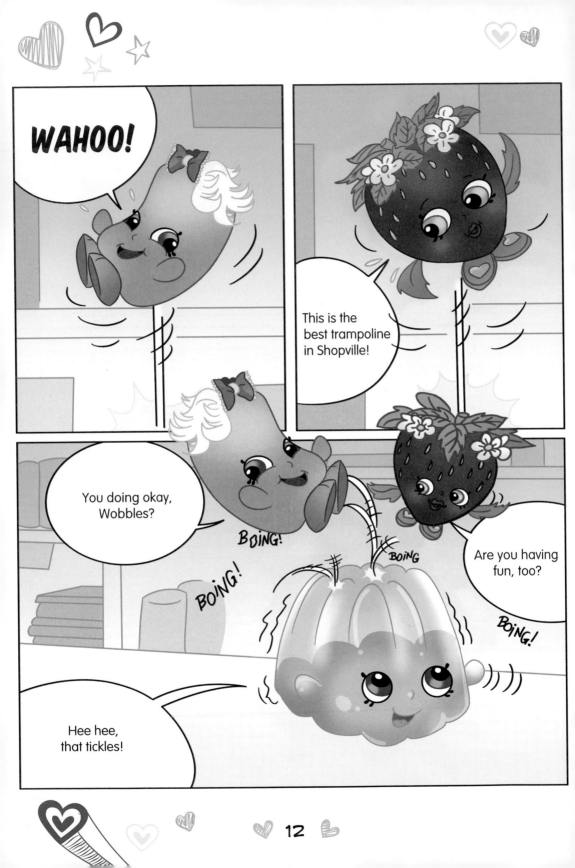

I'm finding it hard to relax today.
With all these bright lights, I can't find a nice dark spot to take a nap.
Isn't there a way to turn down the lights in here?
Ta-da! Sleep well! Hee hee.
Ha ha! Thanks, Gran Jam!

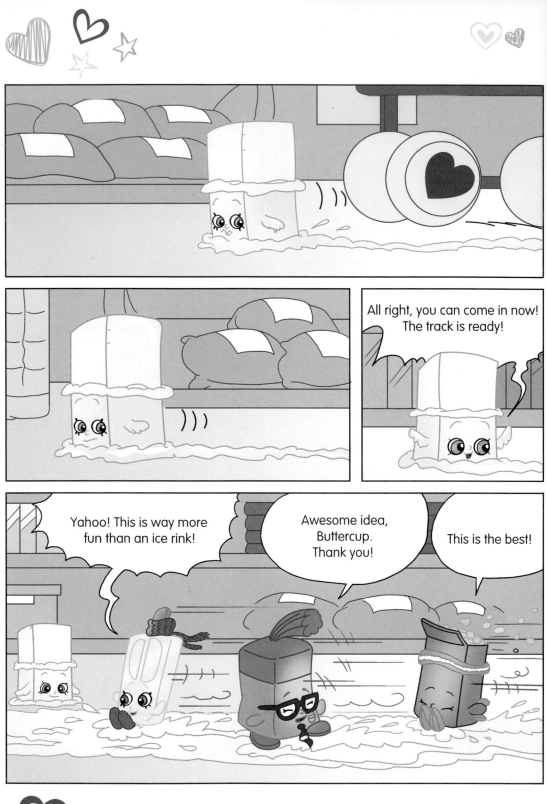

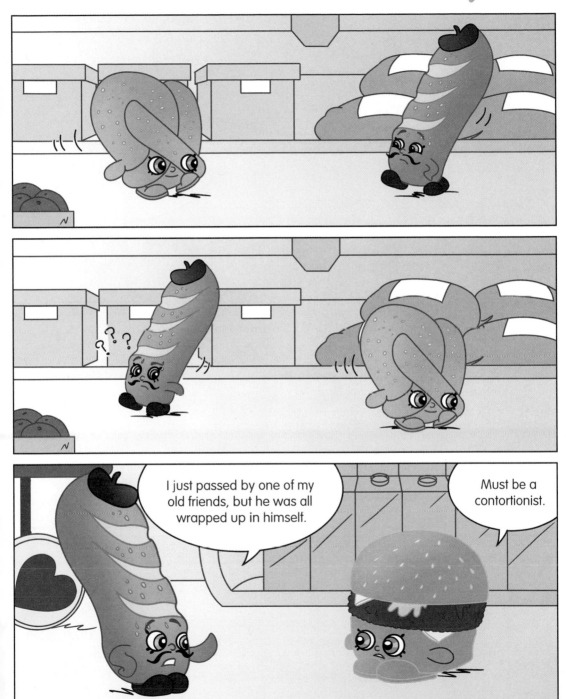

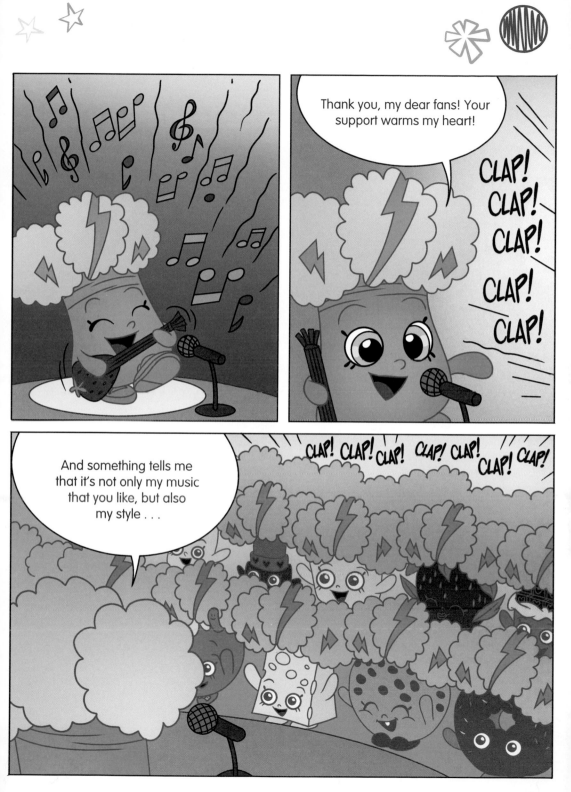

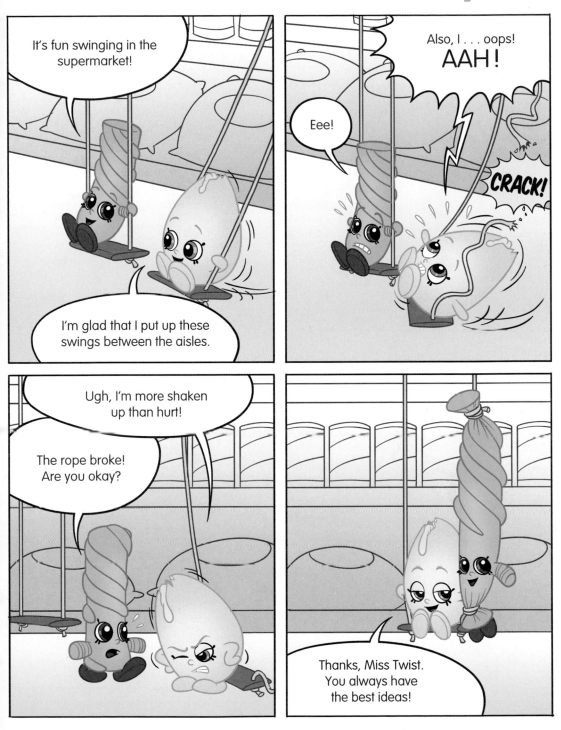

 45

 51

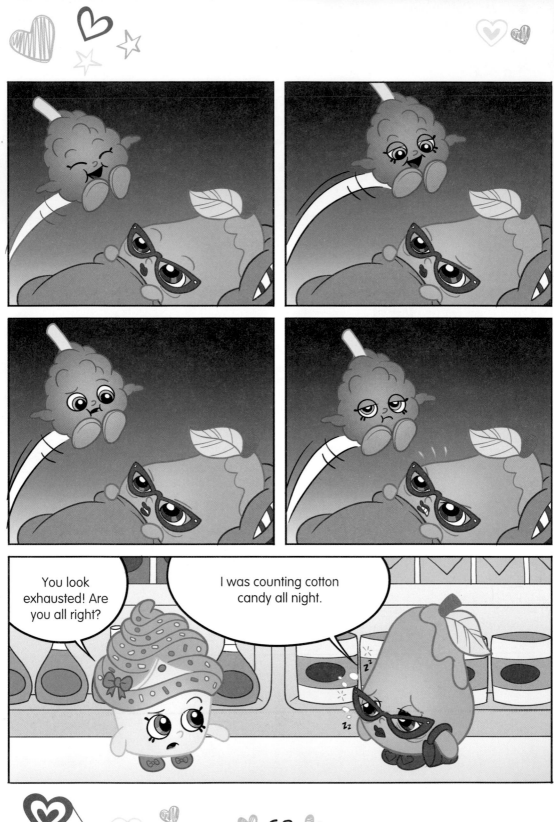

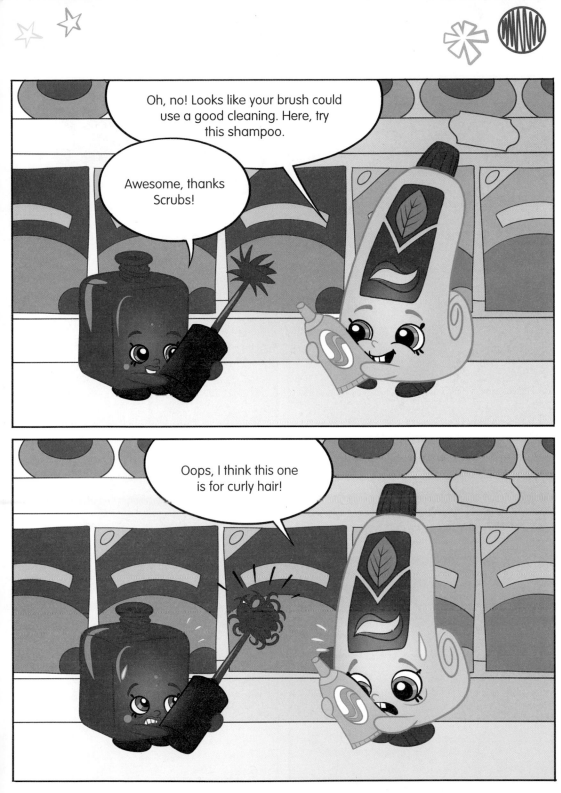

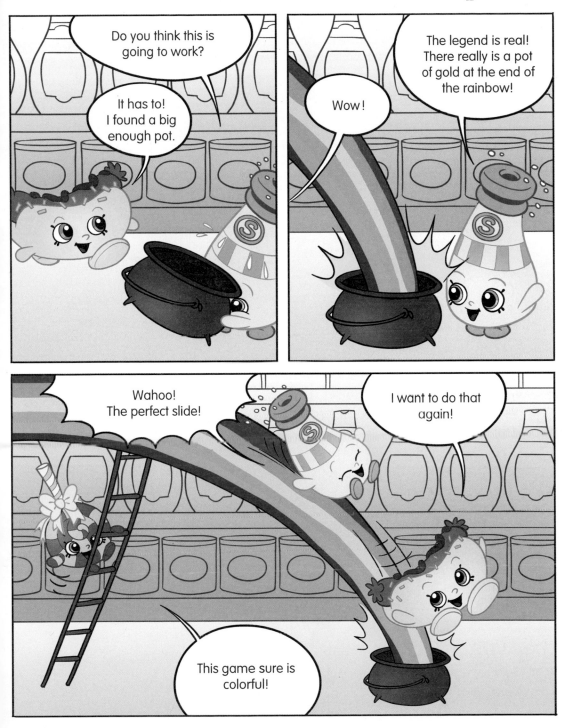

PUNNY JOKES

There's no doubt that the Shopkins know a thing or two about food!

There's no limit to what Chee Zee can *fondue*!

Q. What do Cheeky Chocolate's friends call her when she gets overheated?

A. Hot cocoa!

Apple Blossom is a great problem solver—she really knows how to get to the *core* of the issue!

D'Lish Donut can't help herself from snacking often. It's like her stomach is a bottomless hole!

Q. What's Kooky Cookie's dream?
A. To work hard and make lots of dough!

Q. What's Spilt Milk's biggest pet peeve?
A. When the ending of a movie gets spoiled!

Q. Why is Bubbles always the most festive?
A. Because she loves to have a *ball!*

When it comes to delicious frosting, Wishes truly takes the cake!

Q. What does Gran Jam do when she feels tired?
A. She loves to *spread* out and nap!

Q. What is Poppy Corn's secret dream?
A. To be a famous pop star!

Q. Why can't Wobbles ever hide how she's really feeling?
A. Because you can always see right through her!

Popsi Cool is very dedicated— once she starts something, she'll always *stick* to it!